TREE OF SONG

poems by

Federico García Lorca

Barcelona, 1935

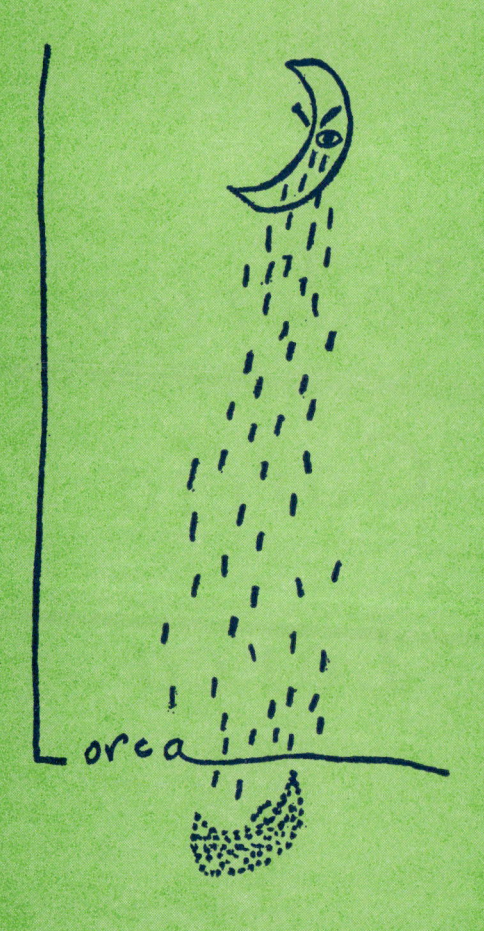

POEM AND PAINTING

Moon above,
moon below,
Lorca in between.
Sky and water
meet
in the soil
of your body.
You painted with blues and greens
your tender little picture,
so tender,
that it will live forever.

Unicorn Keepsake Series

NHAT HANH
Translated by the author and Helen Coutant

BORIS PASTERNAK
Translated by George L. Kline

FEDERICO GARCIA LORCA
Translated by Alan Brilliant

JOHN HOWARD GRIFFIN
Twelve Photographic Portraits

FEDERICO GARCIA LORCA

Tree of Song

TRANSLATED FROM THE SPANISH

BY ALAN BRILLIANT

GREENSBORO UNICORN PRESS 1973

TRANSLATION COPYRIGHT © 1971 BY
ALAN BRILLIANT

Published by arrangement with New Directions Publishing Corporation, agents for the Estate of F. García Lorca. Some of these translations appeared in *Road Apple Review*, *Trace* and *Unicorn Folio*. The drawing and poem used as frontispiece are from Lorca's *Dibujos*.

Second printing: Summer, 1973

UNICORN PRESS
P.O. Box 3307
Greensboro, North Carolina

PQ
6613
.A763
A17
1971b

TABLE OF CONTENTS

Arbol de Canción
Tree of Song

Adelina de Paseo
Adeline of the Street

Cazador
Hunter

Canción de Jinete
Rider's Song

Refran
Proverb

Balanza
Balance

Canción de las Siete Doncellas
Song of the Seven Virgins

La Canción del Colegial
Song of the Schoolboy

Canción del Mariquita
Ballad of the Ladybug

Al Oído de una Muchacha
Confiding in a Girl

La Luna Asoma
The Moon Sails

ARBOL DE CANCION

Caña de voz y gesto
una vez y otra vez
tiembla sin esperanza
en el aire de ayer.

La niña suspirando
lo quería coger;
pero llegaba siempre
un minuto después.

¡Ay sol! ¡Ay luna, luna!
un minuto después.
Sesenta flores grises
enredaban sus pies.

Mira cómo se mece
una y otra vez,
virgen de flor y rama,
en el aire de ayer.

TREE OF SONG

Reed of voice and gesture
once and once again
trembles hopelessly
in the air of yesterday.

The sighing girl
wanted to grasp it:
but always arrived
a minute later.

Ay, sun! Ay, moon, moon!
a minute later.
Sixty grey flowers
tangled around her feet.

See how she sways
once and once again,
virgin of flower and bough,
in the air of yesterday.

ADELINA DE PASEO

La mar no tiene naranjas,
ni Sevilla tiene amor.
Morena, qué luz de fuego.
Préstame tu quitasol.

Me pondrá la cara verde
—zumo de lima y limón—
tus palabras—pececillos—
nadarán alrededor.

La mar no tiene naranjas.
Ay, amor.
¡Ni Sevilla tiene amor!

ADELINE OF THE STREET

No oranges in the sea,
no love in Seville.
Tawny girl, what fiery glances:
lend me your parasol!

I'll make my face green
—lime and lemon juice—
your words—minnows—
swimming around.

No oranges in the sea.
Ah, love.
No love in Seville.

CAZADOR

¡Alto pinar!
Cuatro palomas por el aire van.

Cuatro palomas
vuelan y tornan.
Llevan heridas
sus cuatro sombras.

¡Bajo pinar!
Cuatro palomas en la tierra están.

HUNTER

High pines!
Four doves fly through the air.

Four doves
twist and turn.
Their four shadows
carry wounds.

Low pines!
Four doves lie on the ground.

CANCION DE JINETE

Córdoba.
Lejana y sola.

Jaca negra, luna grande,
y aceitunas en mi alforja.
Aunque sepa los caminos
yo nunca llegaré a Córdoba.

Por el llano, por el viento,
jaca negra, luna roja.
La muerte me está mirando
desde las torres de Córdoba.

¡Ay qué camino tan largo!
¡Ay mi jaca valerosa!
¡Ay, que la muerte me espera,
antes de llegar a Córdoba!

Córdoba.
Lejana y sola.

RIDER'S SONG

Cordova.
Away and all alone.

Black mount, huge moon,
olives in my saddlebag.
Although I know the roads
I will never reach Cordova.

Through the wild, through the wind,
black mount, red moon.
Death's on the lookout
from the turrets of Cordova.

Ay, the road is endless!
Ay, my pony's great heart!
Ay, death awaits me
before I reach Cordova.

Cordova.
Away and all alone.

REFRAN

Marzo
pasa volando.

Y Enero sigue tan alto.

Enero,
sigue en la noche del cielo.

Y abajo Marzo es un momento.

Enero.
Para mis ojos viejos.

Marzo.
Para mis frescas manos.

PROVERB

March
flies past.

And January goes on so long.

January
goes on in sky's night.

And below March is one moment.

January,
for my old eyes.

March,
for my cold hands.

BALANZA

La noche quieta siempre.
El día va y viene.

La noche muerta y alta.
El día con un ala.

La noche sobre espejos
y el día bajo el viento.

BALANCE

The night always quiet.
The day comes and goes.

The night dead and deep.
The day with a wing.

The night above mirrors.
And the day below wind.

CANCION DE LAS SIETE DONCELLAS
(TEORIA DEL ARCO IRIS)

Cantan las siete
doncellas.

(Sobre el cielo un arco
de ejemplos de ocaso.)

Alma con siete voces
las siete doncellas.

(En el aire blanco
siete largos pájaros.)

Mueren las siete
doncellas.

(¿Por qué no han sido nueve?
¿Por qué no han sido veinte?)

El río las trae,
nadie puede verlas.

SONG OF THE SEVEN VIRGINS
(THEORY OF THE RAINBOW)

Seven virgins
singing.

(An arc across the sky:
patterns of sun's setting.)

One soul with seven voices
seven virgins.

(In the light air
seven stately birds.)

Seven virgins
dying.

(Why not nine?
Why not twenty?)

The river bears them,
no one can see them.

LA CANCION DEL COLEGIAL

Sábado.
Puerta de jardín.

Domingo.
Día gris.
Gris.

Sábado.
Arcos azules.
Brisa.

Domingo.
Mar con orillas.
Metas.

Sábado.
Semilla
estremecida.

Domingo.
(Nuestro amor se pone
amarillo.)

SONG OF THE SCHOOLBOY

Saturday.
Garden gate.

Sunday.
Grey day.
Grey.

Saturday.
Blue arcs.
Breeze.

Sunday.
Sea's edge.
Boundaries.

Saturday.
Trembling seed.

Sunday.
(Our love turns
yellow.)

CANCION DEL MARIQUITA

El mariquita se peina
en su peinador de seda.

Los vecinos se sonríen
en sus ventanas postreras.

El mariquita organiza
los bucles de su cabeza.

Por los patios gritan loros,
surtidores de planetas.

El mariquita se adorna
con un jazmín sinvergüenza.

La tarde se pone extraña
de peines y enredaderas.

El escándalo temblaba
rayado como una cebra.

¡Los mariquitas del Sur
cantan en las azoteas!

BALLAD OF THE LADYBUG

The ladybug's dressing her hair
in her silk dressing gown.

The neighbors snicker
out their back windows.

The ladybug commands
each curl to its place.

The parrots purveyors of planets
screech through the patios.

The ladybug reeks
with a sinful perfume.

Combs and hairnets
litter the afternoon.

Striped like a zebra
scandal hovers over the scene.

The ladybugs of the South
sing from the rooftops!

AL OIDO DE UNA MUCHACHA

No quise.
No quise decirte nada.

Vi en tus ojos
dos arbolitos locos.
De brisa, de risa y de oro.

Se meneaban.
No quise.

No quise decirte nada.

CONFIDING IN A GIRL

I wouldn't
I wouldn't tell you anything.

I see in your eyes
two crazy little trees.
Smiling, intriguing, golden.

They are stirring.
I wouldn't.

I wouldn't tell you anything.

LA LUNA ASOMA

Cuando sale la luna
se pierden las campanas
y aparecen las sendas
impenetrables.

Cuando sale la luna
el mar cubre la tierra
y el corazón se siente
isla en el infinito.

Nadie come naranjas
bajo la luna llena.
Es preciso comer
fruta verde y helada.

Cuando sale la luna
de cien rostros iguales,
la moneda de plata
solloza en el bolsillo.

THE MOON SAILS

When the moon sails
bells disappear
and the roads appear
impenetrable.

When the moon sails
the sea covers the land
and the heart feels
isolated by infinity.

No one eats oranges
under the full moon.
Better to eat
green and frozen fruit.

When the moon sails
with a hundred matching faces,
silver money
sobs in its purse.

PRINTED AT *UP* UNICORN PRESS

This second printing of Federico García Lorca's early lyrics incorporates corrections in the translations and the original texts, which have been reset, in 14-point Perpetua, in both Spanish and English.

The type was set by Alan Brilliant and Don Winter (Los Angeles Type Foundry). The book was hand-printed by Eric Smith and Dean Stewart. The cloth edition was hand-bound by Karen Meece and Sharon Bangert. Teo Savory is the editor of the Unicorn Keepsake Series, of which this is Volume Three.

DATE DUE		
MAR 14 1990		
NOV 1 1991		
NOV 3 1998		
DEC 7 19		
GAYLORD		PRINTED IN U.S.A.